To Harper, my sister that I love so much- Bailey
When I Became a Big Sister

Paperback ISBN: 979-8-218-35515-9
Text Copyright © 2023 by Bailey Butler and Christina Dix
Illustrations Copyright © 2024 by Bailey Butler and Christina Dix
Cover Design by Christina Dix; Illustrations by Nalar Studio
Library of Congress Cataloging-in-Publication Data TXu002381941 / 2023-07-06

Published in United States by Bailey Wailey Publishing LLC
P.O.Box 922439
Norcross, Ga 30010
www.baileywailey.com

Printed in the United States of America
2024- First Edition

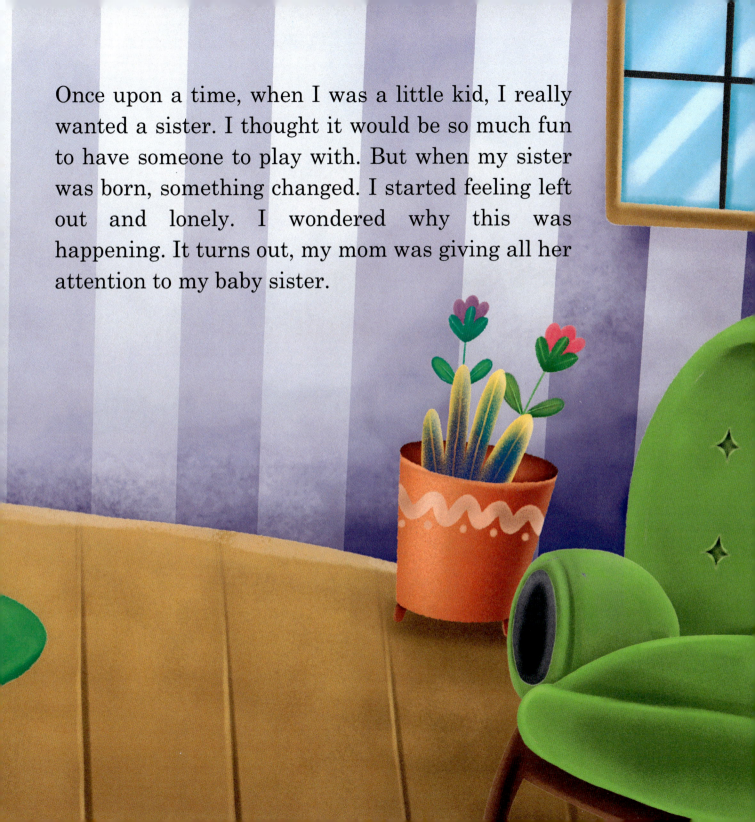

Once upon a time, when I was a little kid, I really wanted a sister. I thought it would be so much fun to have someone to play with. But when my sister was born, something changed. I started feeling left out and lonely. I wondered why this was happening. It turns out, my mom was giving all her attention to my baby sister.

I talked to my mom about how I felt. I told her that I wanted more attention too. She listened to me and said, "Okay." That made me happy, and I went to bed thinking things would be different the next day. But when I woke up, my mom was still giving my baby sister more attention. It made me feel sad.

You might be wondering how my mom was giving my sister more attention. Well, whenever I tried to talk to my mom, she would ignore me and play with my sister instead. It made me feel left out and lonely all over again.

Then one day, my mom took me to my basketball game. Afterward, we came home and watched a movie together. As I sat there with my mom, I started thinking about all the fun things we do together. I realized that my mom wasn't ignoring me after all. She does give me attention, but I wasn't used to sharing it with my sister.

You see, babies can't do things by themselves. They need their mom's and dad's attention too, just like me. Babies can't change their diapers or clothes, and they can't feed themselves. They rely on their parents to take care of them and show them love.

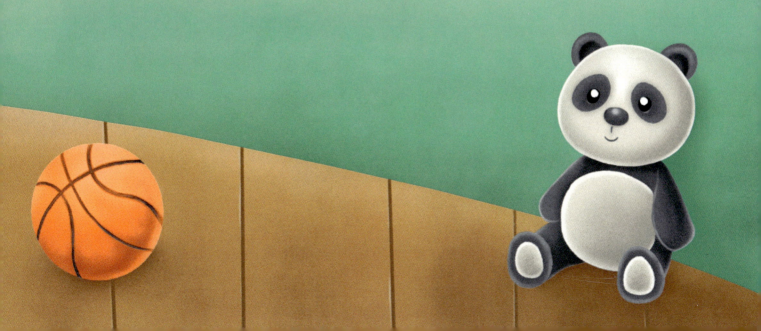

I learned that it's okay to share the attention with my baby sister. Sometimes babies need more attention because they can't do anything for themselves. So now, I play with my baby sister and try to make her laugh. I read books to her since she can't read yet. I give her lots of kisses and hugs. I help my mom change her diaper, and I sing her songs. I always check on her to make sure she's okay.

You know what? I no longer feel lonely. I love having a baby sister and being a big sister. It's a special bond that I cherish. So, if you ever feel a little left out when your parents give attention to your baby sibling, remember that babies need lots of love and care. It's okay to share the attention and help take care of them. And you'll see, being a big brother or sister can be pretty awesome!

Now that I've learned how to share the attention with my baby sister, I've become even better at being a big sister. I want to share some tips with you so that you can be an amazing big brother or sister too!

First tip: Be a role model for your younger sibling. They will look up to you, so it's important to set a good example. Behave responsibly, be kind, and treat others with respect. Show them how to be a good person by your actions.

Next, spend quality time with your siblings. This shows them that you care. Play games with them, watch movies or baby TV shows together, and do activities they enjoy. By spending time together, you'll build a strong bond.

Remember to be patient with your younger sibling. They are still learning and growing. Don't expect them to know everything. Instead, teach them and share what you know. You can help them say their first words, teach them how to ride a bike or swim, or help them with their homework if they are a little older.

Lastly, protect your siblings. As an older sibling, it's your responsibility to keep them safe. Look out for them and defend them from harm. Be their superhero!

By following these tips, you'll be an amazing big brother or sister. Your younger sibling will be lucky to have you! Keep spreading love and being the best sibling, you can be.

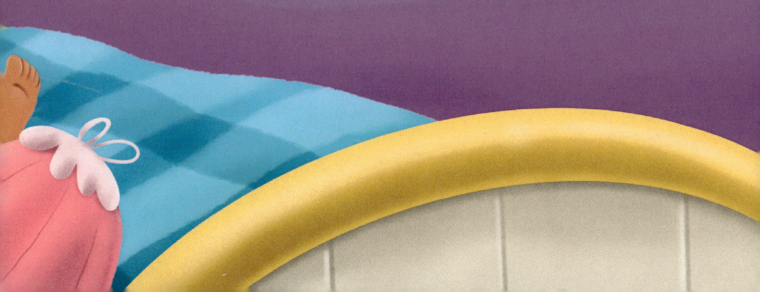

Made in the USA
Middletown, DE
10 September 2024